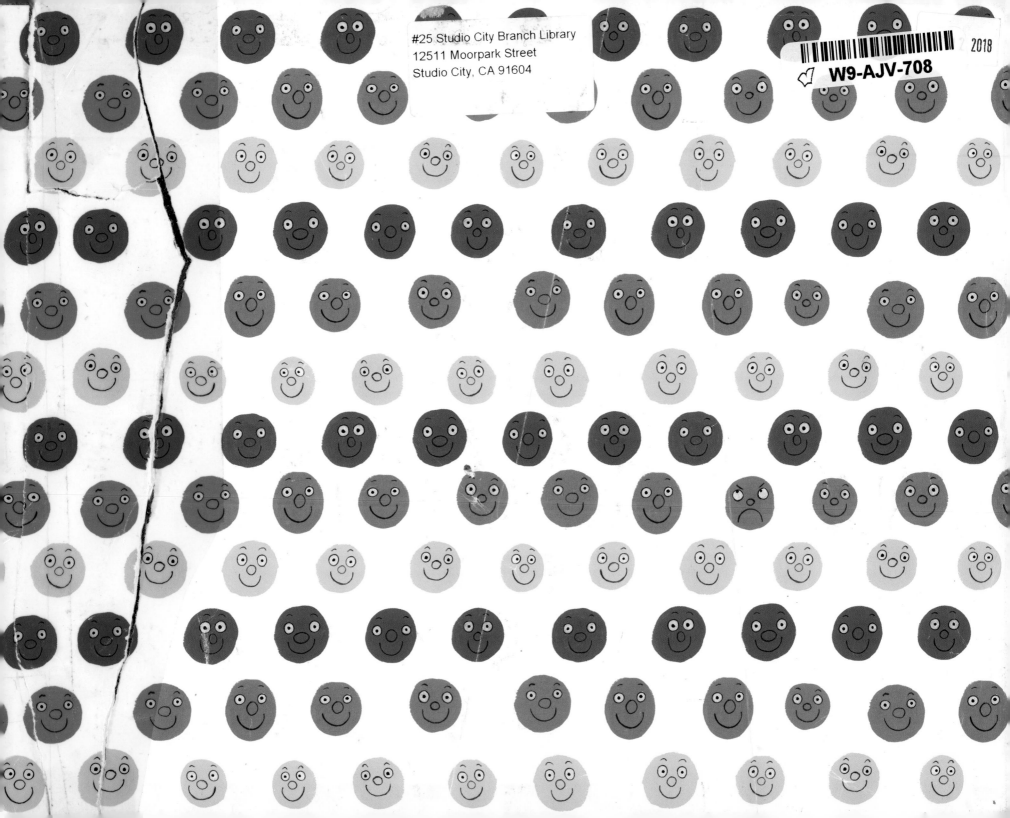

For James, Diego, Emma, Peregryn, Juniper,
Dyson, Kate, Jayden, Hailey, Zoey, and every
new hue mixed into the spectrum

Henry Holt and Company, *Publishers since 1866*
Henry Holt® is a registered trademark of Macmillan Publishing Group, LLC
175 Fifth Avenue, New York, NY 10010 • mackids.com

Copyright © 2018 by Arree Chung

Library of Congress Cataloging-in-Publication Data
Names: Chung, Arree, author, illustrator.
Title: Mixed : a colorful story / Arree Chung.
Description: First Edition. | New York : Henry Holt and Company, 2018. |
Summary: Each believing that their hue is the best, the three primary colors live in
separate parts of the city until Yellow and Blue meet, fall in love, and decide to mix.
Identifiers: LCCN 2017044231 | ISBN 9781250142733 (hardcover)
Subjects: | CYAC: Color —Fiction. | Segregation —Fiction. | Toleration —Fiction. |
Interracial marriage —Fiction. | Racially mixed people —Fiction.
Classification: LCC PZ7.C4592 Mi 2018 | DDC [E] —dc23
LC record available at https://lccn.loc.gov/2017044231

Our books may be purchased in bulk for promotional, educational, or business use.
Please contact your local bookseller or the Macmillan Corporate and Premium Sales Department
at (800) 221-7945 ext. 5442 or by e-mail at MacmillanSpecialMarkets@macmillan.com.
First edition, 2018 / Design by Rebecca Syracuse
The artist used black India ink with brush and acrylics on Rives BFK paper to create the illustrations in this book.
Printed in the United States of America by Worzalla, Stevens Point, Wisconsin
3 5 7 9 10 8 6 4 2

MIXED

A Colorful Story

Arree Chung

Henry Holt and Company • NEW YORK

In the beginning, there were three colors:

Yellows,

Reds,

and Blues.

Reds were the loudest,

Yellows were the brightest,

and Blues were the coolest.

Everyone lived in color harmony. Until . . .

. . . one afternoon,
when a Red said,

The Yellows disagreed.

No! We're the BEST because we're the BRIGHTEST!

The Blues were too cool
to even respond.

The colors decided to live in separate parts of the city.

YELLOW HEIGHTS

But then, one day, a Yellow noticed a Blue.

And something happened.

Yellow and Blue became inseparable.

Life felt so vibrant!

But not all the colors were happy about it.

But Yellow and Blue loved each
other so much, they decided to

MIX!

Together, they created a new color.

They named her Green.

Green was bright like Yellow

and calm like Blue,

but really she was
a color all her own.

Everyone was fascinated.

Even the grumpy colors
fell in love with Green.

The colors began to see new possibilities.

Soon other colors mixed,

and mixed,

and mixed,

and mixed!

There were so many new colors. And a lot of new names.

The old neighborhoods of Redville, Blue Town, and Yellow Heights didn't make sense anymore. Everyone wanted to live together, so they rebuilt the city.

The new city was full of color.

It wasn't perfect.

But it was home.